A FORTUNATE NAME

The *Cousins Quartet*
by
Margaret Mahy,

published by Doubleday:

Available now

The Good Fortunes Gang
A Fortunate Name

Forthcoming

A Fortune Branches Out
Tangled Fortunes

TRANSWORLD PUBLISHERS LTD
61–63 Uxbridge Road, London W5 5SA

TRANSWORLD PUBLISHERS (AUSTRALIA) PTY LTD
15–25 Helles Avenue, Moorebank, NSW 2170

TRANSWORLD PUBLISHERS (NZ) LTD
3 William Pickering Drive, Albany, Auckland

DOUBLEDAY CANADA LTD
105 Bond Street, Toronto, Ontario M5B 1Y3

Published 1993 by Doubleday
a division of Transworld Publishers Ltd

A catalogue record for this book is available
from the British Library

A Vanessa Hamilton Book

ISBN 0 385 40168X

Set in 14/17pt Bembo by Falcon Graphic Art Ltd.
Wallington, Surrey.
Printed in Great Britain
by Mackays of Chatham Plc, Chatham, Kent

J.37,26l
£8.99

MARGARET MAHY

A FORTUNATE NAME

Cousins Quartet: Book 2

Illustrated by John Farman

DOUBLEDAY

LONDON · NEW YORK · TORONTO · SYDNEY · AUCKLAND

To Shirley
— wherever she might happen to be

CHAPTER ONE

From deep in her bed, Lolly Bancroft heard the sound of arguing voices. Or perhaps she dreamed them. She heard (or dreamed) the sound of glass breaking. Was it a real fight, or were television voices coming in under the door? Quick footsteps moved down the hall. She heard an angry, hissing whisper going past her door, but could not make out any words.

Lolly sat up in bed.

'What's wrong?' she called, in a voice all soft and smudgy with sleep.

The angry hissing whisper stopped immediately.

'It's all right, Lolly,' said her father's calm voice. 'Go to sleep, there's a good girl.'

Lolly lay down. Now she knew it was her father outside her door, she felt warm and safe again. Perhaps he had broken something and been cross with himself. She fell asleep almost at once.

When she next woke up, it really *was* morning. The house was completely quiet. Lolly turned over, stretching. *Too quiet*, she thought suddenly, remembering her dream of angry voices and glass breaking in another room.

First, a fierce dream, and now this great silence.

Though a Bancroft morning was never noisy, it was usually filled with polite, gentle sounds. The toaster pinged. The electric kettle purred. Lolly's father, Ivor Bancroft, sorted through his papers which were never bent and grubby like Lolly's pages of homework. *Ivor's* papers made silky, self-satisfied kissing sounds as they touched each other. Not only that: the usual Bancroft morning smelled of bacon and toast. This morning there were no sounds and no smells. The air was empty.

Lolly scrambled out of bed. The silence made her tiptoe as if she were about to creep up on something dangerous. Out of her room she went, and down the hall. Listening hard, her ears felt as if they were stretching out from the side of her head. She opened the living-room door.

A dim light filtered in through the curtains
which were still drawn. The pale, mouse-grey
carpet her father had chosen so carefully gleamed
like silver in the early-morning light. There was
nobody in the room. There were no kitchen
sounds from next door, though the serving hatch
was open. Sun, shining through this golden
peephole, was like light from another world.

As she tiptoed reverently over the mouse-grey
carpet, Lolly felt a sudden, thin pain on the sole of
her right foot. Jerking her foot into the air, a slow
drop of blood fell like a dark tear, leaving a blob
on the carpet. The blood was a wonderful colour,

so dark a red that it looked almost black. Part of Lolly's mind enjoyed the colour, even as she stared in horror. She was standing among tiny, glittering daggers of glass. She was bleeding on to the new, mouse-grey carpet.

Lolly half-expected her father to appear behind her, sighing and shaking his head at her clumsiness. Looking startled and guilty, still holding one foot in the air, she glanced around rapidly and saw that the room had changed since last night. Something was missing. The photograph of her father's mother, the grandmother who insisted on being called Honoria because she so hated to be called Grandmother, had disappeared.

As long as Lolly could remember, that picture had stood on the coffee table, pretending to smile sweetly, but secretly sneering at her. Now, it had gone. Just as well! Honoria Bancroft would certainly have arched her brows and turned down the corners of her mouth at the blood on the mouse-grey carpet. *She doesn't get that clumsiness from the Bancrofts*, the photograph would have said in its wordless way. Honoria said things like that, speaking over Lolly's head as if Lolly would not be able to hear, simply because she was shorter than the adults around her.

There were steps on the outside path and then the click and rattle of the back door opening. The wind chimes hanging in the porch gave out a soft, sweet note. Someone walked through the kitchen. A shadow passed across the golden peephole of the serving hatch. As Lolly stared, the kitchen door opened. Lorna, her mother, came in, wearing yesterday's crumpled clothes as if she had been up all night. Lolly and her mother stared at one another.

'I've just been for a morning walk,' her mother said in a guilty voice. 'Oh, Lolly! What's happened to your foot, darling?'

'I cut it,' Lolly whispered, wobbling as she tried to keep her foot in the air. She could feel a beetle of blood crawling over her heel. 'What's happened? What's wrong?'

'Nothing,' said Lorna, and then she sighed and added, 'Well, something *is* wrong. I'll put a plaster on your foot and have one cup of coffee, and then I'll tell you all.'

'Tell me now,' begged Lolly, feeling herself turn pale with horror. Her father had been killed by a burglar! He had been kidnapped by terrorists from a rival bank! In spite of his sighing and head-shaking, Lolly loved her father dearly and wanted him to live for ever.

'Lolly, darling,' said Lorna, falling to her knees and flinging her arms around her daughter. 'I'm sorry! I'm *so* sorry!'

That settled it. That blood on the mouse-grey carpet, which Ivor had chosen, must be a sign of his death. It had been his ghost speaking at her door in the night. The world whirled. The blood bled.

But Lorna went on.

'Your father and I have had a major fight. Not just one of those polite little Bancroft ones. A real, hot, Fortune fight. I hit him over the head with his mother's picture and he ran off to her at one o'clock in the morning.'

The world still whirled. Her foot still hurt. Lolly felt the safe, solid world around her go all crumbly. At first she was so glad to know that Ivor was still alive that the news was almost a happy surprise. Blood on the carpet was *not* a sign of death, only of divorce. A moment later, the thought of any separation seemed like death of another kind.

'Darling heart!' cried Lorna. 'You're my wonderful girl, but all he ever does is to criticize you. And me! The only person he wants to please is his *mother*. I've had twelve years of it. I've had enough.'

'Bring him back,' Lolly said. 'But I'll clean up the carpet first.'

Her mother hugged her hard. 'Forget the carpet,' she cried. 'Lolly, it's because of me, not you. Look, I've really tried to be a Bancroft for years and years, but I'm not going to try any more. Blow and blast the Bancrofts. I'm going back to being a Fortune again . . . and I'm taking you with me.'

CHAPTER TWO

'You've got to eat more breakfast,' Lorna said.

'You aren't having anything,' Lolly pointed
out.

'That's different,' Lorna said. 'Don't worry me,
Lolly. Eat something.' Lolly did not want her
mother to worry. She drank the orange juice and
ate some muesli. Lorna hovered and flitted like a
protective fairy, straightening things that were
already straight.

At this time in the morning Ivor was usually at
work. In a way, everything was as it usually was
. . . just Lorna, Lolly and breakfast. But
everything felt crumbly. Lolly looked down at
the table top, half-expecting to see thin cracks
creeping across it. It looked perfectly sound.

16

Perhaps it was she herself, Lolly Bancroft, who was crumbling away. She got up from the table, knocking over the sugar bowl.

'Where are you going?' asked Lorna, hastily rescuing the bowl.

'Out to the swing,' said Lolly.

Lolly loved swinging. She was a bold swinger, and swung hard and high, feeling like an eagle or a fighter pilot, or Tarzan, or someone taming the wild horses of the air. If only she were allowed to sit on a swing during her classes at St Joseph's Convent, she felt sure she would always be top of the class.

To her surprise, she found that once she was on the swing, moving backwards and forwards, the crumbling stopped. Perhaps it was because swinging was already full of sudden changes. *Dad's run away from home . . .* down, down, down. *I'm going to be a Fortune not a Bancroft*, up, up, up. No-one had asked Lolly what *she* wanted, but that was the rule of life. Parents did the deciding, and children were decided about. *Go to sleep, Lolly*, her father had said at her door last night, and in a way she felt as if she might still be asleep and dreaming. But, of course, she wasn't.

The swing carried Lolly up again. *I'm going to be a Fortune again, and I'm taking you with me*, her mother had said. Did that mean she would have the name Fortune from now on?

As Lolly swung, she felt herself becoming strong and bold. She was turning into her secret-swing self, Lorelei Fortune, the girl who rode a wild horse of the air. Though Lolly was always called Lolly, she had actually been christened Lorelei, so both names were really hers. But Lolly Bancroft and Lorelei Fortune were like different people. Lolly felt afraid of doing the wrong thing, but Lorelei was always adventurous and brave. If only Lolly could walk away from the swing, carrying Lorelei inside her!

Up went the swing and then down. Down and then up again. Lolly had eleven cousins in town, but not one of them was a Bancroft. Every single cousin was a Fortune cousin. Only Lolly had missed out on that lucky, light-hearted name.

The Fortunes believed they were the greatest family in the world. They stuck together and entertained one another. They celebrated one another's birthdays, had barbecues in one another's back yards, and sang loud, old family songs. Lolly's father, Ivor, watched, smiling politely, but he couldn't join in. He did not know the words. As for Lolly's Fortune cousins, they sang, too, or played hide-and-seek in darkening gardens. But, though Lolly went to all the Fortune parties, her cousins almost never came to visit her. Somehow, the lawns and garden around Lolly's house were too grand for all the trampling and scuffling of a Fortune get-together.

'You think you're too good for us,' one cousin, Tessa, had once said to Lolly. And another cousin, Tracey, had added, 'Your dad thinks he's so great because he's rich. Anyhow, you're not a proper Fortune, not like we are. You haven't got the name.'

Uncle Toby Fortune and his family had come home to Fairfield only six weeks ago, but Pete, the second boy of that new family, was already a member of the gang who met in a tree-house in the forest behind Grandpa Fortune's house. Lolly had lived in Fairfield all her life, but she was still not a member of the gang.

'It's not just a gang. It's a sort of Fortune investment society really,' Tessa would say. 'Only we keep on spending our profit.'

Gang or society, Lolly longed to join in, but no Bancroft could belong to a society (or gang) called the Good Fortunes Gang. And, somehow, to make things worse, Lolly wasn't even a particularly good Bancroft. Honoria was always pointing it out, making Ivor even more anxious about her than he already was.

'You were born with two left feet, Lolly,' he'd sigh and shake his head. When he sighed like that, Lolly wanted to draw herself up and give him a fiery glance.

'Lolly?' she wanted to say to him. 'Lolly's a wet, half-chewed, sugary name. *My* name is Lorelei Fortune.'

'My name is Lorelei Fortune,' Lolly muttered, just to hear how proud and brave it sounded. 'How can you sneak away in the night to Honoria?' she asked Ivor, though he wasn't there. 'Come home at once and things will be all right again. Even better.' The swing swept up so high that she felt she was being swallowed by the sky. 'Much, much better. Things don't have to be the same as they always were. They can get better.' But she could only say that because her father wasn't actually listening.

Then her mother called. She had to get off the swing. Dragging her feet along the ground to slow down, Lorelei felt herself coming back to earth again, though earth was much more uncertain at that moment than the swing. Somehow, her everyday school shoes tied her to the ground. She was Lolly again. She turned around. Lorna was leaning over the veranda, smiling. But the fatherless house behind her seemed suddenly as strange and scary as an unknown forest in a fairy-tale.

$\int 37,261$

CHAPTER THREE

The Fortune cousins had always gone to the state school, Fairfield Primary, but Lolly went to St Joseph's Convent.

'After all, she *is* a Bancroft,' said Honoria, talking over Lolly's head as usual. 'Say what you like, there's a rough element at the state school.'

When Honoria talked about a *rough element*, it was a way of mentioning the Fortune cousins without actually naming them. Honoria did not like the Fortune family, and sometimes behaved as if she thought Lolly had got her Bancroft blood through wicked trickery.

'Private schools do give that little extra polish. And we *all* agree that Lolly could do with a little polishing,' said Honoria. 'I know her father thinks so.'

Getting her ready for her school polishing, Lorna brushed and plaited Lolly's fairish-brownish hair, smiled into her blueish-greenish eyes, and hugged her, growling and pretending to bite her like a kind and loving bear.

'Lolly . . . none of this is your fault.'

'I know,' said Lolly. 'But life must go on.'

'Right!' said Lorna. 'Now it's school. Bag! Bike! Big kiss for mother. Be good, and off you go.'

All day at school, Lolly had that crumbling feeling as she sat behind her solid desk, with initials of St Joseph's pupils from last year and the year before scratched into it. Lolly watched her writing hand, and imagined her pen, and then the fingers holding it, beginning to powder and drift down on to the paper like dust. Later, when she was making an owl-mask for her part in a school play, it seemed as if her eyes were watching someone else's hands draw the feathers.

I'm here but I'm *not* here, thought Lolly. She put on the owl-mask and looked through the owl eyes. But behind the mask, her face felt as if it were smoothing itself out, becoming quite blank like an egg. Quickly she took the mask off again.

That afternoon, when school was over, Lolly put her bag on the carrier on the back of her bike, and her owl-mask in the basket on the front. The mask stared up at her, looking rather frightening. She turned it face down. Then, instead of biking straight home as she usually did, Lolly set off in the opposite direction. She went down Hill Street, through the little Hill Street Park, and into dangerous territory. She waited by the park gate as kids from the state school went by.

There, far down the street, came her cousins, Trace the Ace and her younger brother, Jackson, both on their skateboards. Even from a distance Lolly could see how cool Tracey looked, gliding serenely towards her, skilfully jumping the skateboard over uneven places in the footpath, swinging out around two other children who were merely walking. Tracey's pale hair flashed like a distant signal. Funnily enough, from a distance she reminded Lolly of Ivor, driving through Fairfield traffic in his Jaguar car. Once behind the wheel of his car, he stopped looking anxious and became serene, as if he were gliding across all the troubles of the world.

Two boys, swinging their packs at one another by the park gate, stopped when they noticed a convent blazer. Then they put on posh voices and began to walk with mincing steps.

'Convent cats, stink like rats!' they sang to each other. There was a rule that that was what the state school said to the private school. The boys waited, grinning, for her to shout back at them. Lolly knew she should reply with a well-known rude rhyme about the state school, but the words turned dusty in her mouth. Over the years, Honoria had somehow managed to turn Lolly into a whisperer, and there's not much point in whispering a rude rhyme. However, the boys thought her silence meant that she really did believe she was better than they were.

'You're spying on us, convent cat,' one of them growled, his grin fading.

Just as it seemed the boys might actually do some serious bullying, there was a rush of wheels. Tracey was upon them.

'Leave her alone, creeps!' she shouted. 'If you touch her, the whole Fortune family will gang up on you and that means *me*, Trace the Ace!'

'We weren't going to touch her,' said one of the boys. They hurried out of Tracey's reach. Tracey spun her skateboard on its back wheels. Jackson copied her.

'What are you doing here, Lollipop?' Tracey demanded scornfully. 'Convent cats get killed here. Their skins are hanging from fences all down this street. Go back where it's safe!'

'I was looking for you,' said Lolly. 'I had something to tell you.'

'Go on, then,' said Tracey impatiently. 'Tell us!'

'What, what what what what what?' muttered Jackson, strumming, then drumming the air. Watching Jackson was like watching an entire band riding on a single skateboard.

'I think I'm going to be a Fortune, too,' Lolly said. 'I mean, *really* a Fortune. I think I'm going to be *called* Fortune — like you.'

'How?' asked Tracey. She looked interested. 'Is Uncle Ivor changing his name? Cool move!'

'No,' said Lolly. 'Mother and Dad are separating.'

'Real Fortunes don't get separated,' said Tracey, sounding as if she were stating a universal rule, like the law of gravity. 'They mate for life like weasels. Is it weasels?' she asked Jackson.

'You know . . . on that nature thing on television, it said that *something* mated for life.'

'Swans and geese,' said Jackson, dancing a little. He could actually dance on a skateboard. 'But what about Prue?'

Prue was Tessa's big sister. She had already been married, had a baby, and been divorced. All this had happened to Prue before she was twenty.

'It was weasels,' said Tracey. 'Anyhow, Prue doesn't count. She ran away to get married and she didn't invite any of us. But real Fortune marriages, which everyone's invited to, stick like superglue.'

'But *Lolly* isn't a real Fortune,' said Jackson. He turned to her. 'You don't know the words, man. You haven't got the action, man.' He called everybody 'man', even the Fortune babies.

'Are your parents really splitting?' asked Tracey.

Lolly nodded, hunching her shoulders. She shivered slightly.

'They had a big fight last night,' she said.

'Well, tell Lorna she can get half the house and half the Jaguar,' said Tracey. 'That's the law. She's allowed to get half of all that Bancroft stuff. Don't let him con her out of the Jag.'

'He's already got it,' Lolly said. 'It is *his* car. I mean, he's allowed to have what he loves most.'

Tracey looked grim.

'OK, then why doesn't he have you?' she asked. 'My father sells cars, but he doesn't sell us.'

'Mothers get the kids and fathers get the cars,' Jackson sang. 'That's the law of nature from Mercury to Mars.' He was quick with rhymes, and thought he might be a rap singer one day.

'Giving up the Jag!' cried Tracey, looking suddenly horrified. 'Hey, I'm going to check up on your rights with Sharon Bluett. Her mum's been divorced *twice*.' She began to glide off, with Jackson following her. 'If anything else happens, get on the blower and let us know,' she called over her shoulder. Then she stopped, tilted the skateboard with her back foot, and spun it around so that she was facing Lolly again. 'Hang in there,' she called. Spinning round a second time, she glided off without saying a proper goodbye. Lolly stared after her.

She had not expected Tracey to be sympathetic. Tracey was never sympathetic. But it came as a shock to find Tracey was more worried about the Jaguar than about anything else. The world around Lolly seemed to crumble a little more. She had to find a safe place quickly, or she would crumble, too. She decided to visit another cousin – Tessa.

CHAPTER FOUR

Tessa's sister, pretty Prudence, was warming a
baby's bottle in the kitchen and talking to her
boyfriend, Christopher Moody. As usual,
Prudence was wearing weird clothes . . . a very
short dress which seemed to be made of purple
sacking with coffee-coloured lace sewn around
the bottom, and tights she had painted with
smiling silver skulls and red toothbrushes.

Christopher Moody was watching her with
fascination. He was so respectable himself, it was
hard to believe he could be in love with Prue.

'Prudence Fortune has ruined her life,' Honoria
used to say, looking pleased. However, for
someone with a ruined life, Prudence seemed
extremely cheerful. Her baby daughter was

sitting on the floor in a jumpsuit which Prudence had painted with golden birds.

'Lolly Bancroft!' said Prudence, smiling. 'What are you doing in *this* part of town?'

'Is Tessa here?' Lolly asked in her soft, Lollyish voice.

'In her room, reading up on interest rates,' said Prudence.

Lolly did not know which room belonged to Tessa. She and her cousins mostly met at Grandpa Fortune's house.

When she did find her, Tessa really was checking the interest rates. She had spread the financial pages of the paper all over the floor, and had outlined some of the figures in red.

'Hey!' she said, looking at Lolly in amazement. 'What are *you* doing here?'

She was surprised in the same way that Tracey had been surprised, because Lolly had never come looking for her before. But Tessa was glad to have company, and began immediately to talk.

'I'm going to make an investment,' she cried. 'I've got to make sure I get the best interest, but some places only want your money if you've got five thousand dollars.'

'I've got something to tell you,' said Lolly. 'I'm going to be a true Fortune, after all. I mean, my name's going to be changed to Fortune.'

'Hey! Why?' asked Tessa, staring.

'My parents are separating. They had this great fight,' said Lolly. 'Mother hit Daddy with Honoria's . . . with Grandmother Bancroft's picture.'

'Gosh!' exclaimed Tessa. 'Your mother's getting divorced from a *Bancroft*?' She ran to the door. 'Prue . . . hey, Prue! You're not going to be the only divorced one in the Fortune family. Auntie Lorna's getting a divorce . . . she's getting a divorce from a *Bancroft*.' The news echoed through the entire house.

'What?' yelled two voices. Feet hurried towards them from two directions. The first one through the door was not Prudence but Auntie Marama.

'Lolly,' she said, 'what did you say? Is Lorna actually getting a divorce?'

Lolly had not imagined telling anyone except Tessa.

'They had a fight,' Tessa was shouting. 'Auntie Lorna hit Uncle Ivor with an oil painting of old lady Bancroft.'

'A photograph,' whispered Lolly, but Tessa was making up her own story.

'A Fortune is divorcing a Bancroft,' Tessa went on. 'No-one else would divorce a *Bancroft*. Everyone else would suck up to them because they're rich. But we divorce them.'

'Oh, Lolly . . . how awful,' said Aunt Marama, giving Lolly a kind look. 'Oh, I am *so* sorry . . .' She hugged Lolly. Tessa paused, suddenly unsure of herself.

'We're sorry but *interested*,' said Prudence. 'Don't worry, Lolly, I'll bet you anything they get back together again. I reckon Ivor's crazy about Lorna.' Tessa stopped looking unsure, and began shouting again.

'Christopher, did you hear that? A Fortune is divorcing a Bancroft.'

'Shut *up*,' said Auntie Marama, grabbing Tessa's shoulder and shaking her.

But Prue only grinned. She winked at Tessa
and Lolly as she and her mother quickly set off to
the kitchen to distract Christopher from brooding
about divorce instead of thinking of marrying
Prue.

Tessa sighed, as if the excitement was all over,
and looked back, a little wistfully, at the financial
columns of the newspaper, spread out on the
floor.

'Do you know what?' she said. 'I have saved up
. . . one hundred dollars. *One hundred dollars!*' she
repeated in a hushed, religious voice. 'I've just got
a bank statement. One hundred dollars. It's
nothing to do with the cousins. They spend all
their capital. This is all my own money. I've
saved up pocket money, I've done baby-sitting
for Prue, I've even done *gardening*, and I didn't
spend one single solitary cent of my birthday
money! I saved it all! And my bank statement
came in the post today, and I have got . . . wait
for it . . . I have *one hundred dollars*! Tah *dah*! And I
want to invest it. Do you know about things like
that? I mean, Uncle Ivor manages a bank so
perhaps . . .'

Lolly was shaking her head. Tessa sighed.

'I started watching the money programme on

television,' she said. 'You know, the one that comes on just after the news.'

'I don't watch that,' Lolly said. 'My father does . . . I mean he used to . . . I mean . . .'

'You have to keep watching it,' Tessa explained, 'and after a while you begin to understand it. And do you know what? Money's like a sort of game. I mean, it's serious, but like a video game, too. And if you're rich you're the boss of the world.'

'Well, at our school they say money doesn't buy happiness,' Lolly said, but she could hear herself sounding uncertain.

'Well, I reckon it *helps*,' said Tessa. 'If I had money I'd get a Macintosh computer, and a horse with a paddock to graze it in, and I reckon that would make me pretty happy. I was going to ask Uncle Ivor about investing, and now he's gone, just when I need him. Blast!'

She looked over at Lolly almost shyly.

'I've actually saved a hundred and three dollars,' she said. 'I've got three dollars of car-cleaning money in a vase in my room. Let's spend it. Let's go and get something to eat . . . not anything expensive, but three dollars' worth of something.'

Lolly could see that Tessa was suddenly imagining what it must be like to have no father.

'Ice cream or chips?' she asked.

'Ice cream,' said Lolly.

Walking to a corner shop with Tessa, a few minutes later, and choosing a cherry-chocolate-chip ice cream, made the world seem almost solid again.

CHAPTER FIVE

'I don't know why you had to rush off and tell everyone else in the family,' said Lorna.

They were sitting at the veranda table eating giant hamburgers — something they would never have done if Ivor had been at home. Out on the lawn, the swing was surrounded by a warm, golden halo of late-afternoon sunshine.

'I wanted to tell the cousins that my name was going to be Fortune from now on,' said Lolly.

'Oh well, I don't know about *that*,' said Lorna, looking flustered. 'I hadn't thought quite as far ahead as that.'

'You said you were going back to being a Fortune and taking me with you,' said Lolly accusingly.

'Well . . .' Her mother looked a little bothered. 'Well, I wish you'd waited a few days until . . . Well, never mind,' she said. 'Did anyone ring while I was getting the hamburgers? Honoria? Your dad?'

'No!' said Lolly.

It was curious how much bigger the table on the veranda seemed with Ivor gone. It seemed to stretch for miles. Her father had a way of sitting at the table, staring into space as if he were seeing something more interesting in the distance. At such times he was there, but *not* there. Now, it was the other way round. He was *not* there, but there . . . there on the other side of the table where his space was . . . he was still invisibly watching them. Lolly tried not to look at his empty place.

The phone rang. Lorna got to her feet and walked casually through the glass doors that opened on to the veranda. Lolly could see her mother was trying not to run.

'This is Lorna Fortune,' Lolly heard her say in a cool, elegant voice. Then there was a silence. 'Lolly,' she called, 'it's for you. I think it's Tracey.'

Tracey, thought Lolly. Tracey had never rung her before, but then they were both only getting used to the idea of using the phone. Lolly and her mother passed each other in the doorway, Lorna coming out again, Lolly going in.

'This is Trace the Ace,' said a voice in Lolly's ear. 'Listen, you don't want to be a child of a broken home with no car, do you?'

'We've got my mother's car,' said Lolly.

'But that's just an Escort,' Tracey cried scornfully. 'Dad sells hundreds of them . . . well, he sells a few anyway. Listen, Lolly . . . *are* you listening?'

'Yes,' said Lolly meekly.

'You tell your mother . . .' Trace paused. 'Tell her that children from broken homes don't do well at school. And convents are cruel to them because the Pope isn't into divorce. Tell her that. Are you listening?'

('Tracey!' Aunt Tiffany was yelling in the background. 'Dinner's ready! Get *off* that phone!' Lolly could also hear the noise of small cousins quarrelling and crying.)

'I can't tell her that,' murmured Lolly. 'She'll worry.'

'Make her worry,' exclaimed Tracey. 'She ought to worry.' ('All right! All right! I'm *coming*,' she yelled at someone saying something behind her.) 'Got to go now. Catch up with you later!' And she quickly hung up.

Lolly wandered back on to the veranda. In one day she was not only a child of a broken home, but being given good advice by Trace the Ace.

The phone rang again. Once again Lorna leaped up. However, once again the call was for Lolly.

'I think it's Tracey again,' called Lorna rather crossly.

Lolly and her mother passed each other in the doorway, Lolly going in, Lorna going out. It was not Tracey. It was Tessa.

'Listen,' she began. 'Do you think Uncle Ivor would give me good investment advice now he's getting divorced from us?'

'I think so,' said Lolly doubtfully.

'Yes, but suppose he gives me bad advice out of revenge,' said Tessa.

'I don't think he'd do that,' said Lolly. 'He likes giving good advice.'

'Well, I've been thinking about it,' Tessa went on, 'and you know what? Hang on to him. Uncle Ivor, I mean. We haven't got another bank manager in the Fortune family. We're OK on second-hand cars, and crane hire, and property deals, but we need a banker. Tell your mother.'

'Tell her what?' Lolly asked. 'Stay married to him because he's a bank manager?' She was surprised at her own voice. She sounded a little like Tracey. No! She sounded like Lorelei Fortune.

'Make it sound more sort of . . . romantic,' said Tessa. 'Hang on a minute!'

There was silence as Tessa tried to think of good, romantic things for Lolly to say to Lorna.

'Tell her your father's crazy about her,' she said

at last. 'But don't tell her Prue said it. Just say everyone *knows*. And tell her to think of the family, stuck without good, free advice on investment.'

Lorna was still sitting at the table, staring into space. How could she suddenly bring the conversation round to love and free advice on investment, Lolly wondered. The phone rang again.

'You get it this time,' Lorna said. 'Everyone wants to talk to you this evening, and nobody wants to talk to me.'

Lolly went inside to answer the phone.

'Lorelei Fortune,' she said in a cool, elegant voice, copying Lorna.

'Lolly, dear,' said her father. He sounded tired and sad. He did not sound irritable. 'What sort of a day have you had?'

'I don't know,' Lolly said. It was true. She didn't quite know. The day had begun with invisible crumbling, yet the afternoon had somehow become filled with a sort of sad excitement. Now, hearing her father's voice, Lolly wished he were safely at home — standing on his own mouse-grey carpet and grumbling about the bloodstains, instead of being on the other side of the town with Honoria. She wanted

to talk to him, to ask him something, but she
didn't quite know what it was she wanted to ask.

'Dad,' she began, but he interrupted her.

'Is Lorna there?'

'It's for you,' Lolly shouted to her mother.

'About time, too,' said Lorna.

They passed each other in the doorway, Lolly
going out, Lorna going in.

'Hello,' Lolly heard her say. Then she said, 'I've
got nothing to say to you.' And she hung up.
Lolly stared at her mother, realizing Lorna had
been waiting for Ivor to ring, just so that she
could tell him she had nothing to say to him. It
seemed like a fight at school.

As evening was falling over the garden, Lolly
sat on the swing once more, swinging the sun
down. Lorelei-Fortune thoughts rushed into her
head and filled it to overflowing. What did her

father think of all this? Lorelei Fortune wondered.
Up she went, hanging for a dizzying, wonderful
moment. Ask, she told herself. Is Prue right? Was
Ivor really crazy about Lorna? It was easy to think
about parents liking each other, but hard to
imagine them crazy with love, like soap-opera
people. Only yesterday, Lolly had heard Ivor
complaining because the whole fridge smelled of
fish soup. Do people complain about old fish soup
to people they're crazy about? Ring Dad and ask
him! Down she went, and then up once more.
Yes! Ring him and ask him. Ask him if he wanted
to be divorced. Tell him that she wanted him to
come home again. Simple. It was a Lorelei
Fortune-idea. Lolly carried it safely back across
the lawn, up the veranda steps and into the house,
and it actually seemed as if, this time, Lorelei
Fortune left the swing and walked into the house
with her.

CHAPTER SIX

Lolly had wanted to talk to her father all day —
but with no-one else listening in. She knew that,
if she rang him at work, he would be too busy to
speak to her. Besides, she didn't want to wait
until tomorrow. Ring him at once, now you've
thought of it, advised Lorelei Fortune. There was
nothing for it. Lolly would have to ring her father
at her grandmother's house.

She lay awake, waiting until her mother was in
bed, and then ran softly downstairs and dialled
Honoria's number. She imagined Ivor, unable to
sleep, pacing backwards and forwards, missing
Lolly and crazy about Lorna — even though she
sometimes left old fish soup at the back of the
fridge. He might be longing to be telephoned and
told that he could come home again.

No such luck! It was Honoria who answered the phone.

'It's Lolly,' said Lolly, and then corrected herself. 'It's Lorelei. Could I talk to Dad, please?' She felt pleased with herself because she did not whisper.

'Your father's in bed, asleep,' Honoria said. 'I'm certainly not going to wake him. He's had a terrible day. Not that I'm going to get mixed up in any of this, Lolly, dear. I'm not going to let anyone turn me into a wicked mother-in-law.'

Someone spoke in the background.

'You should be in bed, Lolly,' Honoria said. It was her turn to whisper, or so it seemed to Lolly. 'It's very late. Ring in the morning. Good night, dear.' Then she hung up.

It must have been Ivor talking in the background, thought Lolly. So he was *not* in bed. Honoria just did not want her talking to him. But why not? Lolly stood there, frowning to herself. 'She wants him back,' murmured Lorelei Fortune, 'but I'll bet he doesn't really want to be there. He can't want to live with Honoria more than he wants to live with us.'

The telephone rang right beside her. Lolly leaped with the shock of its shrill cry. Ivor had rung back. He couldn't wait to speak to her!

Spinning around quickly, Lolly accidentally knocked the phone off the little table it stood on. Crouching, she grabbed up the receiver.

'Lorelei Fortune,' she said triumphantly. A voice was whispering on the other end of the phone.

'I can't hear,' Lolly hissed. Her father must be whispering so that Honoria wouldn't hear him.

'Did you tell her what I told you to tell her?' someone asked. It wasn't her father. It was Tracey. 'What did she say?'

Lorelei Fortune invented quickly. 'Mother said a lot of children come from broken homes and live happily ever after. She said it was better for me not to live with a lot of fighting going on.'

'She got that from television,' said Tracey indignantly. 'I heard them saying that on that programme about violence in the home.'

A door opened noisily.

'What on earth's going on?' called Lorna. 'Who's that on the phone?'

Lolly heard someone shouting at Tracey, too.

'She means it's better for *her*,' Tracey said in a hurried mutter. 'People say it's better for kids when they mean it's better for them. No sweat! We'll get them together again. My agent will be in touch with you.' And once again she put the phone down quickly before Lolly had time to say anything more.

'It was Tracey again,' Lolly told Lorna. 'She was just ringing to see how I was.'

'Tracey?' cried Lorna. 'Three times in one evening!'

'Only twice,' said Lolly. 'It was Tessa, once. I think it's because I'm a Fortune now,' Lolly added, even though she knew both her cousins really wanted her to go on being a Bancroft. Tracey liked having a Jaguar in the family. Tessa longed for good advice about investing her savings.

The following morning was a Saturday. The phone rang very early. Lorna was the first one to get to it this time, but once again the phone call was for Lolly, who was still in bed. She had never had so many phone calls before in her entire life. Lorna shouted for her, and stamped back to bed herself, grumbling that it was a bit rough to be woken so early on a Saturday morning. Lolly knew, from Lorna's expression, that the caller was not her father. She thought it would probably be Tracey again.

'I've got instructions to give you,' said a strange voice.

'Who is it?' Lolly asked.

'Me,' said the voice. 'Me, Pete!'

It was Uncle Toby's second son, Pete Fortune, another member of the Good Fortunes Gang.

'Tracey said I was to give you your instructions.

Have you got a pen? You'll have to write them
down.'

'Yes,' said Lolly in an efficient voice. Her father
had been very strict about having pads and pens
next to phones. She scribbled with the pen a little
bit, but it knew immediately who was holding it
and the ink would not flow.

'First, you tell your mother you want to go for
a drive to the War Memorial Park after lunch.
And then say that you want to walk on the track
through the gardens,' said Pete. 'Got that? That's
all.'

'Why?' asked Lolly. Thank goodness she didn't need to write down those instructions.

'It's best if you don't know,' said Pete. 'Our gang is going to help you, but we're going to do it in a secret way so that if anyone asks you afterwards, you can say you didn't know anything about anything. Is your mother listening?'

'She's gone back to bed,' said Lolly.

'If she says she will take you, tie a white handkerchief to your gate,' Pete said. 'A secret agent will bike past and check it out later in the morning.' Lolly was sure he meant himself.

'You must learn the instructions by heart, and then swallow the paper. Good Fortunes signing off,' said Pete, and hung up.

At least she didn't have to worry about swallowing the instructions. Lolly felt glad that the pen had refused to write for her.

She stared at the phone. Then, glancing rather guiltily at Lorna's closed door, she picked up the receiver again. She dialled her grandmother's number, shut her eyes and prayed that this time it would be her father who answered the phone.

But once again the voice that answered was Honoria's.

'Lolly, dear,' she said. 'I'm afraid your father's just gone to work. You know him . . . he's so conscientious, even on a Saturday morning. Goodness knows why. No-one thanks him for it.'

There was nothing for Lolly to do but plan to ring again later.

CHAPTER SEVEN

Rather to Lolly's surprise, Lorna agreed quite
cheerfully to the suggestion that they go for a
drive in the early afternoon. Lolly could not find a
white handkerchief to tie on the gate, but she
hung a pale yellow one on a spike. A good agent
would understand. Later, she and Lorna climbed
into the Escort and drove slowly through
Fairfield.

'It's a nice town,' Lorna said. 'I don't see what
Honoria's got to complain about. Shall we call in
on the grandys?' She meant her parents, Grandpa
and Grandma Fortune.

'On the way back,' Lolly said quickly. She
loved the grandys, but once there, Lorna might
settle down with a cup of tea and begin explaining

herself. It could go on for hours. Lorelei Fortune,
down from the swing, and looking at everything
through Lolly's eyes, did not want to wait around
patiently. She wanted action.

It was a beautiful, sunny day. The narrow road
zig-zagged up to the War Memorial and stopped
there in a paved circle, the memorial set in the
middle of it. You could look out over the whole
of Fairfield from here — over the shops, over the
river, and out to sea. You could see the islands on
the horizon.

The memorial stuck up into the sky like a stone
finger asking for silence . . . a stone finger with a
pointed nail. At night it might bend a little and
scratch at the stars. Down the front of the stone
finger ran a list of names — all names of Fairfield
men and boys who had died in wars on the other

side of the world. There were the names of two
Fortunes among them, a great-uncle of Lolly's,
and, higher up, a great-great-uncle. There were
no Bancroft names, but that was because the
Bancrofts had not been living in Fairfield in those
days. Lorna stared out at the distant islands,
looking thoughtful, even sad. From behind a
phone box at the edge of the paved circle, Tracey
and Jackson appeared, grinned and waved at
Lolly, pointing at a track into the park before
ducking down again.

'Let's go for a walk,' said Lolly. They left the
Escort parked in the stone circle and wandered off
along the track into the park. A hilltop wind came
romping to meet them and kept them company
all the way.

'You can't blame your father altogether,' Lorna
began suddenly, as if it were Lolly blaming him.
Then she talked about how hard it had been for
Ivor being an only child, and how Honoria had
not wanted him to leave her and have a family of
his own, and *of course* Honoria was lonely, but it
was partly her own fault. She sneered at all
Fairfield and all Fortunes. She refused to make
friends. She had made life difficult for Lorna for
years and years . . . not in any big way, but in
dozens of little ways that were hard to complain
about. Lolly knew all about Honoria's little ways.
She thought about the night before, and the way
Honoria had pretended Ivor was asleep and
couldn't come to the phone. She glanced back
over her shoulder.

'Why do you keep looking over your
shoulder?' Lorna asked curiously. Lolly did not
realize until then that she *had* been looking behind
her. She couldn't tell Lorna that it was because a
Good Fortunes plan was about to swing into
action. It might come from any direction at any
moment.

'It's time we went home, anyway,' Lorna said.
'Tracey has probably been trying to ring you all
afternoon.'

They reached the car and Lorna started the

engine. But, when they were halfway down the
zig-zag hill, Lolly saw her mother grow suddenly
worried. A moment later she pulled into a
parking bay at the side of the road, slid out, and
walked around the car. Then she came back,
looking cross.

'A flat tyre,' she said. 'What on earth do I do
now?'

'Can't you fix it?' asked Lolly.

'Of course I can. I've got the jack, the wheel
brace, a spare tyre . . . everything I need,' her
mother said. 'But it's so awkward here. The
road's so narrow. Look . . . that tyre's absolutely

flat. The tube must have burst or something.' She smiled at Lolly. 'Don't look scared. It's a nuisance, but no big deal, really.'

Lolly was not looking scared because of the flat tyre. Behind her mother she had caught a glimpse of Pete, Tracey and Jackson peering round the corner, then ducking back out of sight. She was just wondering how this could possibly be part of a Good Fortunes plan when Lorna exclaimed in horror. Lolly turned in time to see her mother leap into the drain at the side of the parking bay and hide herself in some bushes. A moment later a noble car, almost too noble for the War Memorial road, came smoothly around one of the hairpin bends. It was the Bancroft Jaguar, and the driver was Lolly's father. He waved at Lolly. It was almost as if he were expecting to see her standing there, all alone, waiting for him to come and rescue her. He tried to squeeze the Jaguar into the parking bay beside the Escort. There was not enough room for it. Part of it stuck out into the road. Ivor shook his head and leaped out, looking efficient.

'Never mind,' he said. 'This won't take a moment. Where are the car keys? I need to open the boot.'

'I haven't got them,' said Lolly.

'Do you mean your mother went off and left you like this?' asked Ivor. He spoke over Lolly's head, looking left, then looking right. Something had pleased him, but he was slightly puzzled, too. Another car came up the road towards them. Ivor was opening the back of the Escort with a spare Escort key on his key ring. He stopped and held his breath as the other car inched past the Jaguar.

'So your mother's *ditched* you,' he remarked meaningfully. Lorelei Fortune seemed to drain away out of Lolly. She didn't know what to say.

'Gone,' she stammered. 'She's gone.'

'Gone where?'

'Gone to get help,' said Lolly, trying not to look at the ditch behind her.

'Your mother can change a tyre better than I can,' Ivor said scornfully. 'What's she playing at?' All the same, he still looked quite pleased. He jacked the car up, took the wheel off, and put the spare wheel on in its place. It took about ten minutes and that included breath-holding time as other cars inched by the Jaguar. Lolly kept getting glimpses of Tracey and Jackson, first at the corner itself, then on the top of the bank that loomed over the corner. *Now*, she thought. *Now* was the time to talk to her father. *Now* was the time to ask him if he really wanted to live with Honoria. *Now* was the time to tell him that she had tried to ring him twice. *Tell him now*, Lorelei Fortune said. *He's changing a tyre*, Lolly answered, hesitating. *Now*, Lorelei commanded her.

'Dad,' Lolly began firmly, 'I want to ask you something . . .'

'Just a moment,' he said, working at the jack again. The car sank down gratefully on to its new, hard tyre.

Ivor straightened and looked around, frowning.

Lolly took a deep breath.

'Dad,' she began again in a Lorelei Fortune-voice. But he still wasn't listening properly. Instead, he looked scornfully at the bushes that hid the drain. 'Your mother must be feeling remarkably *guilty* about something,' he said. 'I mean, to ring me and then run away.'

The bushes burst apart. Lorna sprang out, her hair full of leaves and twigs.

'I'm here,' she said. 'What a despicable thing to do . . .'

'What do you mean?' Ivor cried.

'Don't deny it,' she shouted back. 'You let the air out of my tyre so you could come gliding by, accidentally-on-purpose, and I'm supposed to be *grateful* to you. But I could have changed that tyre standing on my head.'

'I know you could,' said Ivor. 'So why did you ring me up pretending to be Lolly. Of course I knew it wasn't Lolly!'

'Me? Me ring you?' screamed Lolly's mother.

Lolly opened her mouth. She could see Tracey and Jackson standing on the bank above the phone box, staring over at them, and suddenly Tessa and Pete appeared, too. The whole Good Fortunes Gang was listening in.

There was a sudden roar in the air. A big, rusty car skidded sideways around the corner, its tyres slipping on the narrow road. It was filled with big kids from Fairfield High School . . . six or seven teenagers of all colours. Ivor did not even notice them. The only thing he could hear was the sound of his argument with Lorna.

'Come on! Admit it. You watched us. Then you followed us,' Lorna was yelling at him. 'And while we were walking, you let the air out of my tyre.' She gestured dramatically up the road towards the War Memorial.

'Never! I don't *do* childish things like that. You rang me at the office. You talked in a high voice and pretended to be Lolly, and said you needed help,' Ivor declared. 'And here I am. So what's it all about? Why did you hide?'

'I hid because I didn't want to talk to you,' Lorna shouted.

There was a dreadful, scraping sound. Ivor spun round as the rusty car accelerated, skidded, and vanished round the corner.

Ivor behaved in a way Lolly had never seen him behave before. He howled like a werewolf, then took off after the rusty car though he must have known he had no hope of catching it.

'Quick!' cried Lorna, and pushed Lolly towards their own car.

'But, Mother . . .'

'Quick! Don't argue!'

Lolly stared desperately towards Ivor who had stopped running and was standing in the centre of the War Memorial road with his back to them. There was no sign of the Good Fortunes Gang. The four cousins had faded into the trees on either side of the road. Lolly imagined them running off along the tracks of the War Memorial Park, much faster than members of most gangs or investment societies could run.

Lorna had opened the passenger door of the Escort. Now, she pushed Lolly through it. Slamming the door, she sprinted round to the driver's side. Ivor turned.

'Wait, Lorna!' he shouted. 'Just wait a moment, will you?'

But Lorna was already in the driver's seat. Ivor began to run back down the hill.

'Wait!' he shouted again.

The Escort roared into life. Lorna did some inching of her own. The Escort tilted as she edged out of the parking bay and past the scraped Jaguar. Lolly gasped. But they were through. Off they went, leaving Ivor behind them. Perhaps it was only Lolly who heard his last cry.

'If *you* didn't ring me, who did?'

CHAPTER EIGHT

'Tracey thought that if your mother saw the Jaguar she would be sorry she was separated from your father,' said Pete to Lolly on the phone that evening. 'She unscrewed the cap from your mother's tyre and held the valve open with a nail.'

'She was lucky to find a nail,' said Lolly.

'She brought it with her,' said Pete. 'It has to be the right size.'

'Dinner, Lolly!' called her mother. In spite of the disastrous day, Lorna was looking cheerful.

'Poor Ivor,' she said as they sat down at the dining-room table. 'He loves that car of his. But what a trick to play on us! He must be desperate.' She smiled happily.

Lolly, though, was not so sure. Two whole

days had gone by since her father had left home.
The world was beginning to feel less crumbly.
She must be getting used to a house without him.
Tomorrow morning, Lolly vowed, she would
talk to Ivor properly. Even Honoria would not be
able to stop her.

The next day was Sunday. Lolly got up very
early, and invented a breakfast for herself. She felt
fearless and slightly wicked, stealing the scraps
and putting them side by side on one big plate.
She enjoyed one cold sausage, two kinds of
cheese, three slices of salami, four chocolate
biscuits and an ice cream. Ice cream for breakfast
was a Lorelei Fortune-idea. Then she went out
and got Sunday off to a good start with some
swinging. In its way, swinging was like a sort of
war dance.

It was going to be another beautiful day. The
early sun could not quite reach the swing because
of the Bancroft brick wall. However, the top
branches of the swing-tree were fiery with new
light. Swinging, Lolly tilted her head back, and
looked into criss-cross twigs, growing and
glowing above her. Suddenly dizzy in a
wonderful way — with the rush of the swing and
the light in the branches — she knew that *now* was

the right time. No more telephoning. There had
been too much of that already. She would get on
her bike, ride round to her grandmother's house,
and lurk among the hydrangeas in the garden
until she saw her father on his own. Then she
would leap out of hiding, and ask him things.
Was he really crazy about Lorna? Did he really
want to live with Honoria? And why did he seem
to take Honoria's side so often instead of Lolly's
and Lorna's?

At that hour on a Sunday morning the streets
were empty. The morning light made them
strange and beautiful. Lolly, on the bike, was
almost like Lorelei Fortune on her wild horse of
the air. She was careful, and yet she rode more
swiftly than usual, feeling she was the only
moving Fortune in Fairfield — perhaps the only
moving person in the world. From the basket of
the bike her owl-mask looked up at her. She had
forgotten to finish it, but it still looked really
good, Lolly thought. Its round, empty eyes stared
out of carefully-drawn feathers. Its open beak,
drawn sideways, was fierce and sharp. She
stopped outside an empty timber yard and put it
on. This time her face behind it did not feel like a
peeled egg. It felt suddenly wise. Wearing the
mask, she was freer and wilder than she had ever

been before. A fierce, owl-faced girl was riding through Fairfield to talk to her father — to rescue him! Ivor needed rescuing.

Lolly padlocked her bike to a telegraph pole a little way down the road from Honoria's house. She could see her grandmother's gate was padlocked, too, but that morning Lolly was also Lorelei Fortune. Without hesitating, she climbed over the wall, grazing her knee painfully as she did so. Tracey would have gone over a wall without grazing anything, but Lolly hadn't had much practice wall-climbing . . . not yet. On her hands and knees, the owl-mask catching on all sorts of twigs, she crawled through the hydrangeas. There, framed in wide green leaves, was the front door of her grandmother's house.

Ivor's Jaguar was drawn up, waiting for a driver, its poor, scraped door turned towards her.

As Lolly spied, her father came out and put a folded rug and a basket on to the back seat of the Jaguar. Then he went inside again. Early as it was, she had caught him in the act of setting out somewhere. Lolly's luck was in at last.

She darted across the strip of lawn, which had been clipped and terrified into perfect neatness, opened the door and scrambled on to the floor behind the front seats. When her father came back, Lorelei Fortune would be waiting for him.

But a moment later, she heard Honoria's cool, bleating voice — her words louder as she came closer and closer. Lolly crammed herself down behind the driver's seat, her legs stretched out behind the passenger seat. She would not come out again until they were on the road, with Honoria well behind them. Then she would leap up and say, 'Hi Dad!' — just as cool as Tracey or Jackson.

But the door on the passenger side opened. Wherever her father was going, Honoria was going too. Her grandmother climbed neatly and carefully into the passenger seat.

'Stop worrying!' Honoria was saying. 'She'll get over it. Of course, she will. The Fortunes

might be a little common, but they have plenty of
common sense. And if she doesn't . . . well, dear,
I hate to say this, but it could be a blessed release.'

As she spoke, she pulled the seatbelt strap
across her chest. Her thin, wrinkled right hand
began feeling for the slot between the two front
seats. If she turns, Lolly thought, she'll see me.
She imagined herself taking that searching hand
and guiding it in the right direction. It crawled
backwards like a crab. Its fingers twitched and
tapped within centimetres of Lolly's knee. Then
they twitched and tapped forward, and found

what they were searching for. There was a click. The seatbelt was fastened, and Honoria had not turned around once. She had not even looked down.

Both seats sighed and shifted as Honoria and Ivor leaned back. The car started and moved off with its secret owl-girl hidden behind the driver's seat.

CHAPTER NINE

'A day at the beach will clear your mind,' Honoria
said. 'Don't ring Lorna! Don't run after her.
Don't even think about her.'

The car sped smoothly along. Suddenly, Lolly
felt almost as if she were on the swing. Because
she couldn't see out of the car window, she felt
she was flowing along. Though she was in her
own father's car, he did not know she was there.
Her mother did not know where she was. Her
cousins did not know where she was. Nobody
knew where she was except Lolly herself.
Telegraph wires gently looped past in long,
shallow curves. No wonder she was reminded of
the swing! Up, down and then up again.
Sometimes it seemed as if the wires were actually

flying, swooping gracefully along beside them.

'Mind you,' said Honoria, leaning back firmly, 'I did warn you before you married . . .'

'I don't want to talk about it,' said Lolly's father. 'You just can't be fair to Lorna, Mother, and she can't be fair to you.'

'Oh, so it's *my* fault, is it?' said Honoria. She gave a little laugh. 'I might have guessed it would come to that.'

'It's my fault,' Ivor said quickly. 'I *am* finicky. I complain a lot. I'm always nagging at Lolly for example . . .'

'There's plenty to nag at,' said Honoria quickly. 'It's for her own good, dear. At least *I* understand that. There's a rough element in the Fortune family. You don't want her copying them.'

'Let's forget it,' said Ivor. 'It's a lovely day. Let's enjoy it, if we can.'

'There's more to marriage than a pretty face,' Honoria went on as if he had not spoken.

'I've been married twelve years. I know that,' said Ivor. 'Ma, don't go on about it or I'll turn back to town.'

But Honoria wanted to go on about it . . . on and on and on. She had a gentle voice, but, as she talked, Lolly began to feel sorry for her father.

Honoria said Ivor was all she had, so she couldn't help taking an interest in his life. She was so proud of him. He had done so well, and she wanted to help him. She couldn't help getting angry when she thought he wasn't appreciated.

Lolly stuck out her tongue at the back of the car seat.

'Lorna will see reason,' said Honoria. 'Those Fortunes never give up a dollar if they can avoid it.'

'Ma,' said Lolly's father, sounding tired. 'What's the use of taking a break from my troubles if you talk about them all the time?'

'Was I?' asked Honoria innocently. 'I suppose it's so much in my mind. I can't help feeling for you, after all you've done for them.'

'Let's stop and have a cup of tea, shall we?' asked Lolly's father.

The car swerved left, then right.

'It doesn't look like much of a place,' said Honoria.

'It's the best there is,' said Lolly's father. Then they left the car.

Lolly waited a moment or two after they had gone. She wriggled around, working herself loose again, then very slowly peeped over the edge of the window, and saw the backs of her father and Honoria walking briskly towards a rather dilapidated general store. TEAS, said a notice outside it. Just as well I'm disguised, thought Lolly behind her owl-mask.

She marched boldly into the shop. There her father and grandmother were, sitting at a table in the window looking completely annoyed with one another.

'A double ice cream,' said Lolly loudly. She thought a loud voice would be like a disguise for someone who often whispered. Neither her father or her grandmother looked at her.

'What flavour?' asked the man behind the counter.

'Chocolate ripple on the bottom and hokey-pokey surprise on the top,' Lolly answered.

'I thought it might be a hold-up,' said the man behind the counter, looking at her mask in a puzzled way.

'I have to be disguised,' said Lolly. Then she carried the ice cream back to the car. Even Tracey couldn't have been so cool. No doubt about it, Lorelei Fortune was out and about in the world.

One thing she *was* certain of: her father was not enjoying life with Honoria.

Lolly scrambled into the back of the car and tucked herself and her ice cream down behind the passenger's seat this time, not the driver's seat. Just as she was finishing her ice cream, her father and grandmother came back to the car. Once again the thin fingers twitched close to Lolly's knees as the seatbelt was fastened. Within another moment they were speeding on their way.

'I must say,' said Honoria after a short silence, 'you're not easy to sympathize with, Ivor.'

'Look!' cried Lolly's father. 'You were the one that said I should think about something else. Now, you won't stop talking about it. And it's none of your business.'

'Oh, so it's none of my business?' cried Lolly's grandmother. 'Haven't I done my best over the years? Haven't I been generous to Lorna, and perfectly sweet to the child?'

'What do you mean, "the child"?' cried Lolly's father. 'Her name's Lolly. Call her by her name.'

'Yes! Call me by my name!' Lolly's lips shaped the words. 'My *real* name.'

'Lolly, then,' said Honoria. 'I've always been sweet to Lolly, though it's not been easy. She's a plain little thing, and not too bright. Even you must admit that. She's not real Bancroft material, poor little Lolly.'

But Lorelei Fortune was not plain or poor or little. She was brave and bold and beautiful behind her wise-owl mask. She scrabbled as she bent her knees in the space between the front seats and the back one, pulling her feet in under her, quickly, not clumsily.

'What's that?' cried Honoria, feeling something struggling behind her as if it were battling upward to space and light. Lolly unfolded like a tree, and stood over her.

'Stop calling me Lolly. I'm Lorelei Fortune,' she cried. 'And I *am* bright. I'm *blazing*!'

Glancing back, Honoria saw a fierce owl-face glaring over at her shoulder. She screamed with fear. Through the mask, for the first time in her life, Lorelei Fortune saw Honoria look terrified. It was a wonderful moment — like being high on the swing — and it seemed to pause as if it might last for ever.

'Dad!' she shouted. 'Come home again! I want you at home.'

CHAPTER TEN

Ivor and Honoria could no longer have a picnic with stowaway-Lolly for company. They had to turn round and make for home again.

'I'm sorry to say this about a daughter of yours, dear,' Honoria began, but Ivor stopped her.

'Don't say anything!' he exclaimed.

'Oh, I see,' Honoria cried. 'You're going to defend her, are you? After all I've done for you, you're going to let her frighten me out of my wits. She could have killed me, with my heart the way it is.'

'Ma, please don't start all that again,' begged Ivor. 'You know Doctor Morton says you've got a heart like an elephant.'

For some reason this made Honoria angrier

than anything Lolly could have said or done. She talked in a tight, furious voice, demanding apologies, and a punishment for Lolly. But then, when Ivor did not take any notice, she grew quieter and at last completely silent, staring out at the countryside as if there were nobody worth talking to in the car. Secretly triumphant, Lolly-Lorelei watched the power lines swinging by like thin, black waves.

When they reached Honoria's house, Lolly thought her grandmother would slam the Jaguar door and march inside without saying a word. Instead, she cried in a softer, more desperate voice than her earlier one, 'Ivor, please! Don't make a fool of yourself again.'

'Please don't be so cross, Ma,' said Ivor. 'It's bad for you. After I've taken this monster home, I'll catch up with you later.'

His eyes met Lolly's in the driving mirror, and, to her surprise, he winked at her. He wasn't good at winking, but it suddenly seemed to Lolly that he might improve with practice.

'Well, you certainly frightened the wits out of poor old Honoria,' he remarked as they drove past the hydrangeas.

'I wanted to frighten her,' Lolly said.

'You terrified both of us,' said her father.

'I rang you twice,' Lolly said, 'but she wouldn't let me talk to you.'

The car stopped outside the spiky iron gate in front of Lolly's house. They sat together in the Jaguar, Lolly in the front seat now, beside her father. Her bicycle, shrouded in sacking to protect the Jaguar upholstery, was slumped in the back seat. They were alone together at last.

'She's very lonely, you know,' said Ivor Bancroft at last. 'She was the most important person in my father's life. She wants to be the most important person in mine. She hates taking second place.'

'Are we really important, Mother and me?' Lolly asked. She wanted to hear him say they were.

'Of course you are!'

There was the simple answer to her simple question.

'But your mother mightn't want to stay married to me,' Ivor went on. 'I worry too much to make a good Fortune.'

'You're too disapproving,' said Lolly. Ivor looked startled.

'Well, some things deserve to be disapproved of,' he said.

'You disapprove of fun,' said Lolly. 'Of Fortune fun. You don't sing along.'

'I *don't* disapprove of fun,' Ivor cried. 'But I'm just not a singer-alonger. I'm a listener. After all, singers need listeners, don't they?'

That was true, Lolly thought with surprise. She loved the Fortune family. She longed to be part of the Good Fortunes Gang (or as it might be, investment society), but her very best times were on her own, swinging in silence on the swing. Perhaps that's where Lorelei Fortune worked best, though it was nice to think she could come down from the swing whenever she was needed.

'Come in with me,' Lolly said. 'Come in and tell Mother that you want to stay married to her.'

Ivor laughed.

'She already knows *that*,' he said. 'She's the one who has to make up *her* mind.'

'I'll tell her I *want* you to stay married,' Lolly said. 'I really do. And I'll stop knocking over tea and bleeding on the carpet.'

'Bleeding on the carpet?' Ivor sounded dismayed. 'On the new grey carpet? Did you cut yourself on the broken glass?' Then he laughed a little and shrugged. 'How awful for you, but blood on the carpet doesn't matter . . . not compared with everything else,' he said. 'I'm sorry.'

'You can't help it,' Lolly said. 'It's because of your upbringing. But mostly you're just the right sort of father.'

Ivor did something Lolly was not expecting. He turned towards her and put his arms around her.

'Lolly, dear, you're just right, too,' he said. 'I'll learn to worry less. I learned commercial law. I must be able to learn other things as well.'

'And will you tell Tessa how to invest her hundred dollars?' asked Lolly. Between her grandmother's place and her own house she had explained how she had come to be hiding in the car, and had told him how very much not only she, but other people, too — people like the Good Fortunes Investment Society – wanted him to be part of the Fortune family for ever. Just to prove it, she had even explained how the Fortune cousins had tried to arrange a romantic meeting between Ivor and Lorna through mysterious phone calls.

'Tessa should put her hundred dollars towards the cost of panel-beating the side of my Jaguar,' he said, letting Lolly go again. He took off his glasses and wiped them with his clean handkerchief. He always had a clean handkerchief. The remains of a tear was rolling down the side of his nose. 'But tell her to come into the bank with her hundred dollars and I'll tell her how to get the best interest. I didn't know she was so interested in investment, but you often miss out on important details in big, family get-togethers. When everyone's singing along, you don't hear solo voices, do you? Now off you go inside. I'd better go home and calm Honoria. You scared her out of her wits.'

'I scared her out her wits with my tu-whit tu-whoo,' said Lolly. She and Ivor looked at each other and suddenly burst out laughing at the thought of the fierce owl-girl rising up above Honoria and terrifying her.

'Well, off you go, Lorelei Fortune,' said Ivor once more, this time with a sigh and a smile.

'You said I was more important than Honoria,' argued Lorelei Fortune quickly. 'Come in with me. Please, Dad!'

'But you have a mother and a Fortune family,' Ivor said. 'Honoria's only got me, Lolly.'

'Call me Lorelei,' she said, and for the first time she felt that from now on she would always be Lorelei, even to herself. 'That's the name you chose for me. And don't stay outside like a visitor, Dad.'

'All right, Lorelei!' said Ivor, starting the Jaguar. Its motor purred immediately like a good, obedient cat. They turned in at the gateway in the brick wall, drove past the swing-tree, and drew up outside the veranda, just as Lorna came out to meet them.

CHAPTER ELEVEN

The Good Fortunes Gang always met in a Fortune
family tree-house in the middle of two foresty
acres belonging to Lolly's Fortune grandparents.
Grandpa Fortune was working in the garden as
Lorelei biked through the gate at the foot of the
hill.

'The others are up there already,' he called, just
as if he were used to seeing Lorelei arrive on her
bicycle and climb up the track into the bush. 'Call
in and say hello to us later.'

Lorelei knew just where the tree-house was,
but the Fortune cousins were laughing and
shouting so loudly that anyone could have found
them. A rope with knots in it dangled down from
the tree-house branch, and someone had nailed

slats of wood on to the tree trunk, making a rough ladder.

Standing underneath the tree, she shouted, too. 'It's me!' she cried.

There was silence. For a second, she could hear a bellbird calling, far off among the trees. Then there was a scuffling sound. Tracey looked down from the tree-house, before vanishing again.

'It's Lolly,' Lorelei heard her saying to the others. 'Just because her name's Fortune now, she thinks she can join.'

'My name's not Fortune,' Lorelei shouted. It was funny that, when she was telling them her name was *not* Fortune, her words came out in a real Fortune yell. 'And don't call me Lolly. From now on everyone's got to call me Lorelei or I won't answer.' That was another strange thing. It was her first name not her last that had been changed by the adventures of the past few days.

Tracey walked like a tightrope-walker out on to one of the branches that supported the tree-house. Jackson followed her so quickly it seemed as if they must be wired together.

'Make room!' commanded Tessa, who came next. Then the three of them had to shuffle a long way along the branch to let Pete come out of the tree-house and stand beside them. Pete grinned at

Lolly. He was the only one who was smiling.

'You said your name was going to be Fortune,' Tracey said crossly. 'Make up your mind.'

'I have made it up,' Lorelei said. 'My mother can go back to being Fortune if she likes, but I'm going to be called Bancroft. And Lorelei!'

'Hey! Have they made up, after all?' asked Tessa suddenly.

'Dad came home for a while last night, and I think Mother was pleased to see him,' said Lorelei. 'At any rate they had a cup of tea together, and they laughed twice, and I saw Mother pat him on his shoulder, and then my grandmother, Honoria, rang up to find out where he was.'

'Did he go back to old lady Bancroft?' asked Tracey scornfully. 'What a wimp!'

'Mother *told* him to go,' said Lolly. 'But she wasn't mad with him any more. She was just a bit sorry for Honoria, because I'd jumped out at her and frightened her.'

'Jumped out at her?' cried Tessa. 'You? Why?'

'I'll tell you if you let me join the club,' said Lorelei, cunningly.

'You can't join the club if you're not called Fortune,' said Tracey.

'It's more fun to be a Fortune,' said Jackson.

'Well, I'm making it fun to be a Bancroft,'
Lorelei cried boldly.

'Fun to be a Bancroft? How?' asked Tracey.

'Well, we could build a tree-house in my swing
tree . . . a sort of *branch* meeting place — like you
have branches of banks, but really in the
branches,' Lorelei said. 'And we can have parties
up there.'

The Fortunes on the branch above looked at
each other.

'Now you're here, you might as well come up,'
said Tracey. 'Anyhow, cousins have to stick
together, whatever their names are.'

'We'll be the Good Fortunes Gang *and*
Investment Society, with headquarters *and* a
branch,' said Pete, siding with everyone.

'Mind you, Fortune's still the best name to
have,' said Jackson.

'*Best* and *Bancroft* go better together,' Lorelei
said boldly, and, rather to her surprise, Tracey
grinned and punched Jackson's arm as if to say,
Think about that, man! Then she stretched her
hand down towards Lorelei, who had started to
climb.

As she approached the branch, her left-hand
fingers curled over the edge of the tree-house
platform, and her right-hand fingers wiggled in

the air. Tracey's hand took hers. A moment later, Lorelei was sitting among the cousins, part of the gang at last.

It was wonderful to be there. Her mother and father were getting over their quarrel. She would go home and find them together again, she was sure. And her swing would be waiting for her, ready to carry her up into the air. But that was for later, when she would really enjoy being on her own. Now was the time for being one of the cousins and part of the Good Fortunes Gang, up among the leaves.

THE END